LITTLE TIGER
BIG TIGER

By Lois Hamilton Fuller

Illustrated by Anil Vyas

There was a mother tiger
And her small tiger cub.
They lived near a river
In a shady jungle.

When the sky was dark,
The mother tiger
Hunted for deer and pig.
The tiger cub
Stayed close by his mother's side.

If the Langur monkey saw her
He called a loud, harsh call:
"Watch out! A tiger is coming!"

The Sambhar deer bellowed,

The Kakar deer barked,

And sometimes the game got away.

She hunted then for jungle fowl,

For pheasant and for frog,

Or went to the river for fish.

But she did not hunt every night.

If the moon was bright,
The mother tiger lay down
And waited for the dawn.

She twitched the tip of her tail,
And the tiger cub pounced on her tail
Again and again.

If he went too far away,
The mother tiger called him
With a low, quiet grunt.
The tiger cub came back,
But he did not like
To stay near his mother
In the jungle at night.

One night the mother tiger
Was tired and closed her eyes.

The tiger cub saw a tiny frog,
Hopping along the ground.
The tiger cub pounced,
But the frog hopped away.

He chased the frog and caught it,
And turned to show his mother.
But she was not in sight.

Instead he saw a tiger,
Bigger than his mother,
Near him in the jungle.
The tiger's green eyes glistened
As he watched the tiger cub.
The tiger cub was frightened.
He could not hide or run.
He let the frog hop away.

The tiger crept up closer
To the little tiger cub.

But a roar filled the jungle
The roar of the mother tiger!
She faced the other tiger,
And he went away.

In the daytime,
When the sun was hot,
The mother tiger and the small tiger
Liked to sleep
In the shade of the jungle.

And they liked to swim in the river,
Or rest in the shallow water
On the sand or on a rock.

The mother tiger liked to roar,
A loud, big tiger roar,
To tell all the other animals
In the jungle
That she was there.

All the other animals
In the jungle
Kept far, far away.

The tiger cub liked to roar,
A loud tiger-cub roar,
To tell all the other animals
In the jungle
That he was there.

All the other animals
In the jungle
Were not afraid at all
And none of them ran away.

But there came a year
When the small tiger cub
Was a full-grown tiger.
He walked for miles alone,
Hunting for game at night.

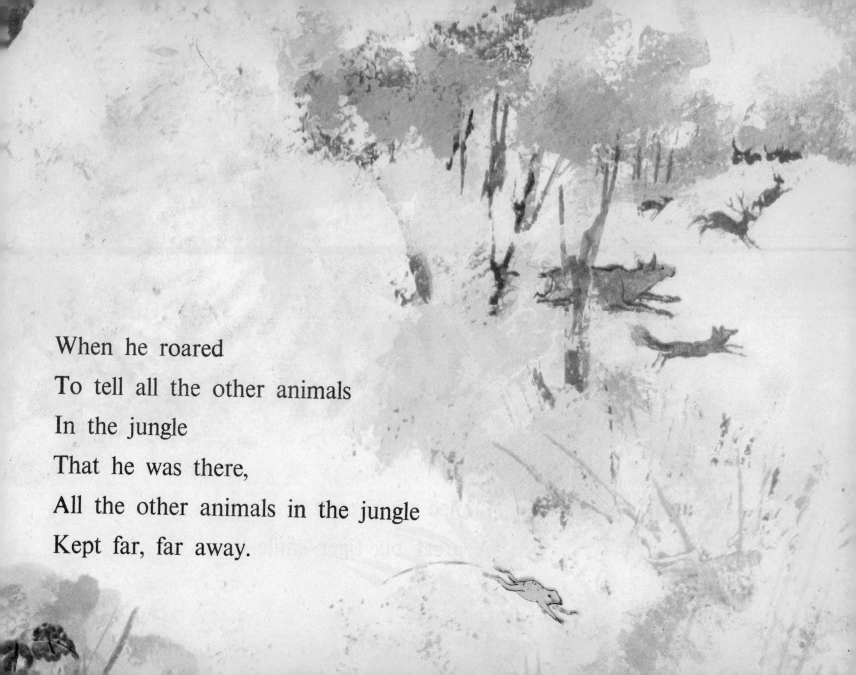

When he roared
To tell all the other animals
In the jungle
That he was there,
All the other animals in the jungle
Kept far, far away.

And the great big tiger
That had been a small tiger cub,
Hearing his own loud roar,

Smiled to himself
A great big tiger smile.